D0230216

There's a monster in my house

Jenny Tyler and Philip Hawthorn

Illustrated by Stephen Cartwright

There is a little yellow duck, a white mouse and a spider on every double page. Can you find them?

There's a **monster** in my house

It's hungry, fierce and fat!

Don't be silly Milly

I think it's only...

There's a **monster** in my house

It's hiding in its den.

Don't be silly Milly

I think it's only...

There's a **monster** in my house

It's massive, huge and big!

Don't be silly Milly

I think it's only...

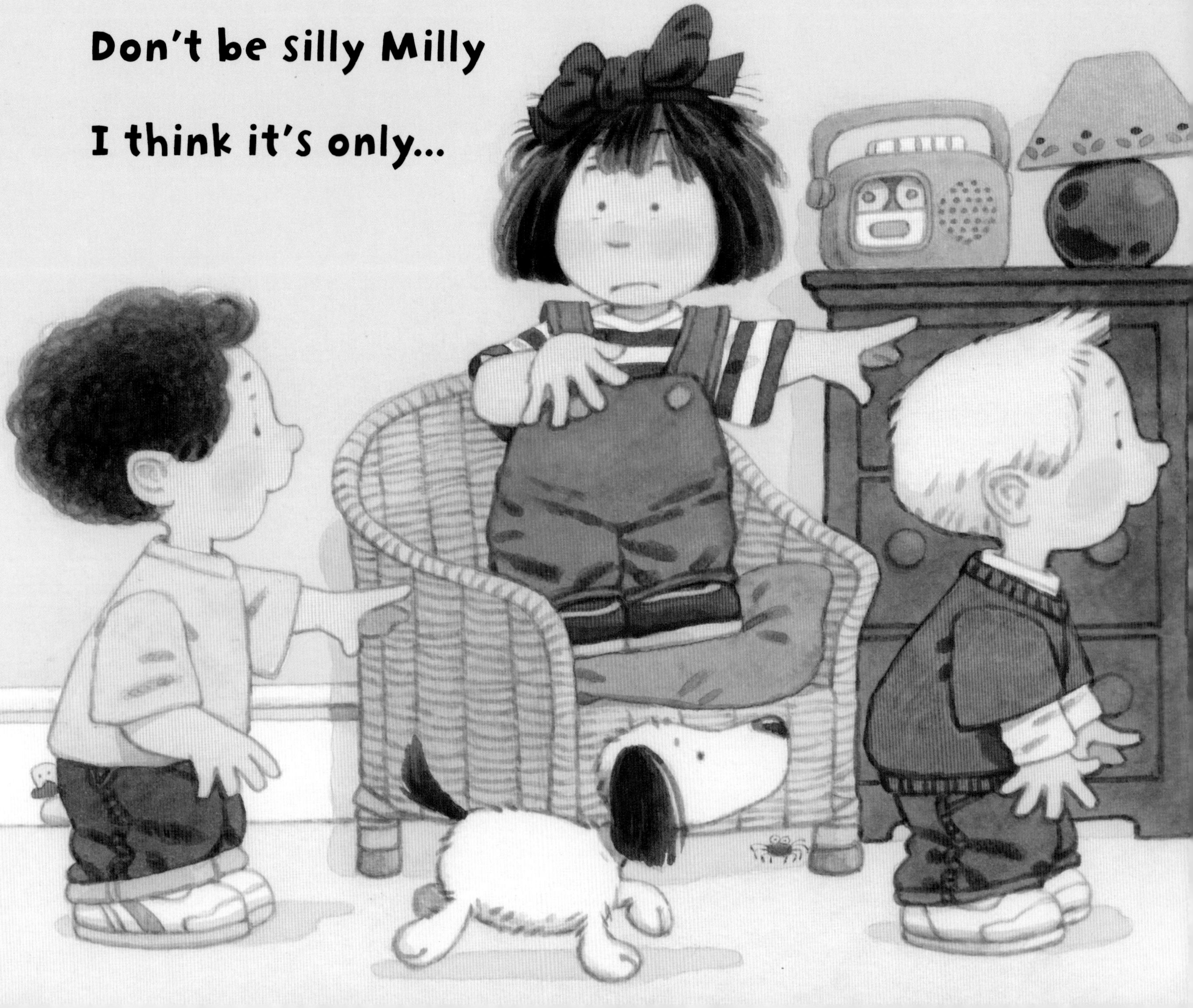

There's a **monster** in my house

It's a Giant Goggle-frog!

Don't be silly Milly

I think it's only...

There's a **monster** in my house

It's chewing up my socks!

Don't be silly Milly

I think it's only...

There's a **monster** in my house

I'm scared to go in there!

Don't be silly Milly

I think it's only...

There's a monster in my shed

It's bound to eat my house!

Don't be silly Milly

I think it's only...

This edition first published in 2006 by Usborne Publishing Ltd., 83-85 Saffron Hill, London EC1N 8RT, England. www.usborne.com

Printed in China
UE. This edition first published in America 2007